...me for Wm self. his... ...assign...

...hereof the following described Slaves for life,

..., named "Edy," aged abou...

...Negro (Son) Boy named "Charles

...declared to be the legal

...ndor,—and being herein fully

...edhibitory vices, defects

...by the Laws of Louisiana

...s were acquired by the

..., in the State of Virginia

...tate recently

...OLINA.

...sents shall come I *Robert F. W. Allston* ___ send, GREETING:

___ in the State aforesaid, *Planter* ___ by my bond or ob-

...noro

...*Robert F. W. Allston* ___ am held and firmly bound unto

...ever *Cato* with these Presents stand held and firmly bound unto

...ecutor of *Thomas Cato* in the penal sum of one thousand fourteen

...coleus Conditioned for the full and just sum of seven Hundred

...ead, in two equal annual instalments with interest payable annu-

...by the said Bond and Condition, reference being thereunto had unto

...edgat large appear the said *Robert F. W. Allston* ___

...payment of the said sum of *Seven Hundred and twenty dollars* ___

___ unto the said *Joseph W. Allston Executor as aforesaid his*

...strators, or Assigns, together with lawful interest for the same, *Have* ___

...oresaid, the following negro slaves to wit *Daniel, John Barton, Kate,*

...d by these Presents *do* bargain and sell, and in plain and open market deliver unto the said *Joseph W. Allston*

Peter. ___ negro slaves ___ Executors, Administrators, and Assigns: forever.

...d to hold the said ___ negro slaves ___

...ph W. Allston Executor as aforesaid his ___ *Robert F. W. Allston his* ___ *Joseph W. Allston Executor as*

...s, or Administrators, shall and do well and truly pay, or cause to be paid unto the said *Joseph W. Allston*

...d his ___ **Days Nevertheless,** That if the said *Robert F. W. Allston* ___ certain Attorney, Executors, Administrators, or Assigns, the full and just sum of

...the true intent and meaning of the said *Bond and Condition* aforesaid, and of these presents, together with lawful interest

...ed of bargain and sale, and all and every clause, article and thing therein contained, shall cease, determine, and be utterly void and of none

...thing herein contained to the contrary thereof in anywise notwithstanding. *Robert F. W. Allston his* ___

it is hereby declared, by and between the said parties, and the said *Joseph W. Allston Executor as*

...do ___ covenant, promise and agree, to and with the said *Joseph W. Allston* ___

...ll happen to be made of, or in payment of the said sum of *Seven Hun-*

...that then, and in such

Freedom over me

*Eleven slaves,
their lives and dreams
brought to life by*

Ashley Bryan

A Caitlyn Dlouhy Book

Atheneum Books for Young Readers • New York London Toronto Sydney New Delhi

At An Appraisement Held at the House of Mrs Fairchilds on the 5th July 1828 to appraise the Property of the Estate of Cado Fairchild Dec'd Disposed of his Will —

One Negro woman Name Peggy	$150-00
one do do Sr Charlott and child	400-00
one Boy name Neptune	300-00
	100-00
	300-00
	175-00
	100-00
	189-00
	864-00
	100-00
	60-00
	1-00
	250-00
	150-00

4494 lot Seed Cotton @ 7½cts pr lb $337-05

3476-5

The Fairchilds

certify the Above To be A Just And True raisement of all the Property Mentioned in the will & Testaments of Cado Fairchilds Dec'd Pro

Mrs. Mary Fairchilds

I mourn the passing of
my husband, Cado Fairchilds.
He managed our estate alone.
Eleven Negro slaves,
they carried out the work
that made our estate prosper.
He never hired an overseer.

My husband apprenticed slaves
to learn trades—
carpentry, sewing,
pottery, basketry, ironwork.

Once our estate was established,
Mr. Fairchilds loaned
our skilled slaves
to neighboring estates.
Their earnings
came to us.
The profits increased the value
of our estate.

Life here without my husband
would be impossible for me.
I trust our Negro slaves,
but I hear stories
of runaways,
of slave insurrections.
I would not feel secure.

I'm having the estate appraised.
After the sale
I will return home
to England,
where I may live without fear,
surrounded by my own
good British people.

At An Appraisement Held at the House of
Mrs Fairchildes on the 5th July 1828 to appraise
the Property of the Estate of Cado Fairchild
Dec'd Disposed of his wife —

One Negro woman Named Rigg and child to Charlott Hill	$150 – 00
			400 – 00
one to do		300 – 00
one Boy named Neptun		100 – 00
one woman Malvina		300 – 00
one Girl Jan		175 – 00
one to Amelia		100 – 00
one Man Dash		189 – 00
21 Large Steurs @ $9 p Hd		864 –
192 Head of Stock Cattle @ $4.30 p Hd		100 –
one Boy Mon		60 –
one Lot of Hogs 40 Hd do		
One Handmill		
one Negro man Named Bacus		250
one woman Betty		15
Lot Jim Cotton @ Hcts pr Pd		3

2 – 50
1 – 50
1 – 00
3
11

For Sale

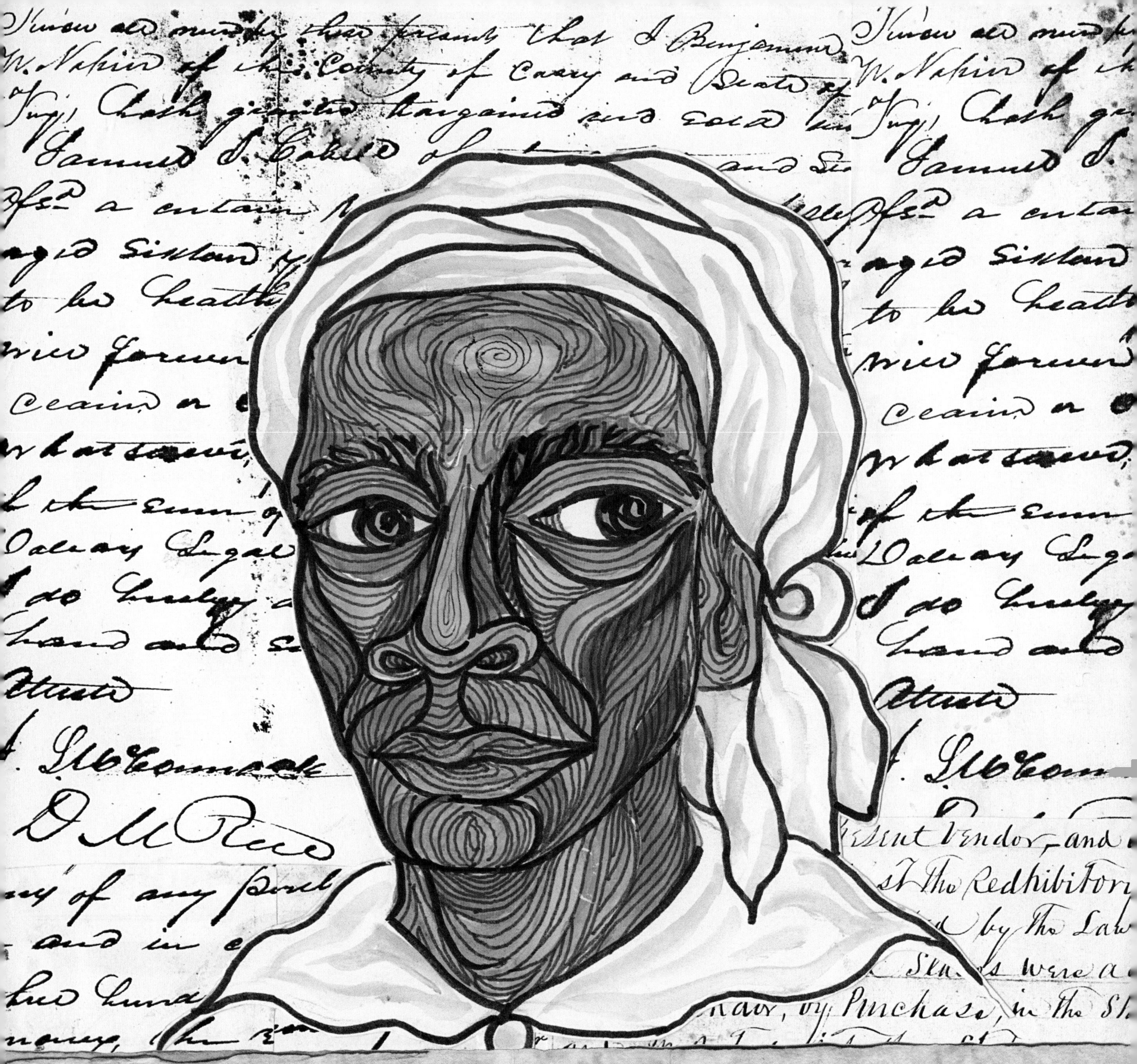

$150 *Peggy, age 48*

Peggy

I am the Fairchilds' cook.
I work in the Big House
day in, day out,
making special meals for the
Fairchilds,
plain foods for the slaves.
Like a field hand,
I work hard—
all profit to the estate.

Mrs. Fairchilds
praises my cooking.
She often chooses a menu
and invites friends
to show off my skills.
Afterward,
I sneak leftover food to the slaves.

As cook to the Fairchilds,
I am free to wander
the estate gardens
and the woods.
I learn about local plants,
plants for cures—
sarsaparilla and chamomile roots,
spruce and buttermilk roots.

The spices I gather
add flavor to the meals
I cook for the household.

Wandering the estate woods
reminds me of the woods
at home in Africa.
Often I re-live that day
our village was raided.
My father was killed,
my mother and I captured,
sold to white slavers.
My mother and I survived
the dreaded crossing to America.
So many others died,
crammed in the filthy holds
of the vessel.

The vessel docked.
We were sold on the block,
no two of a family or tribe together.
Frightened by voices shouting
in no tribal language we knew,
stripped of everything,
our language, our customs,
they even took our names.
They called me Peggy.
Peggy!

I've never again
seen my mother.
Still, I feel close to her,
especially when I steam
roots and herbs
for cures for my slave family.
This stirs ancestral memories—
my roots in Africa.

Peggy dreams

On the Naming Day ceremony
my parents named me
Mariama, "Gift of God."
My parents calling
"Mariama! Mariama!"
sings on in me.

As cook to the Fairchilds,
my room was built
onto the shed
behind the big house.
But no advantages
of working in the Big House
separated me from
my brothers and sisters
working in the fields.

I tell the slave child Dora
stories about each plant.
I teach her basic steps
in cooking well,
just as my mother
taught me.

My knowledge makes me
hunger for more.
Relieving the aches,
the pains,
the suffering
of the slaves
is my chief joy.

When the young boy John
suffered a head injury,
he came to me.
I examined the wound,
then bound a poultice
of roots and herbs
around his head.

Mrs. Fairchilds's dinner guests
praise my cooking.
The praise, however,
that touches my heart
is to hear the slaves
call me Herb Doctor.

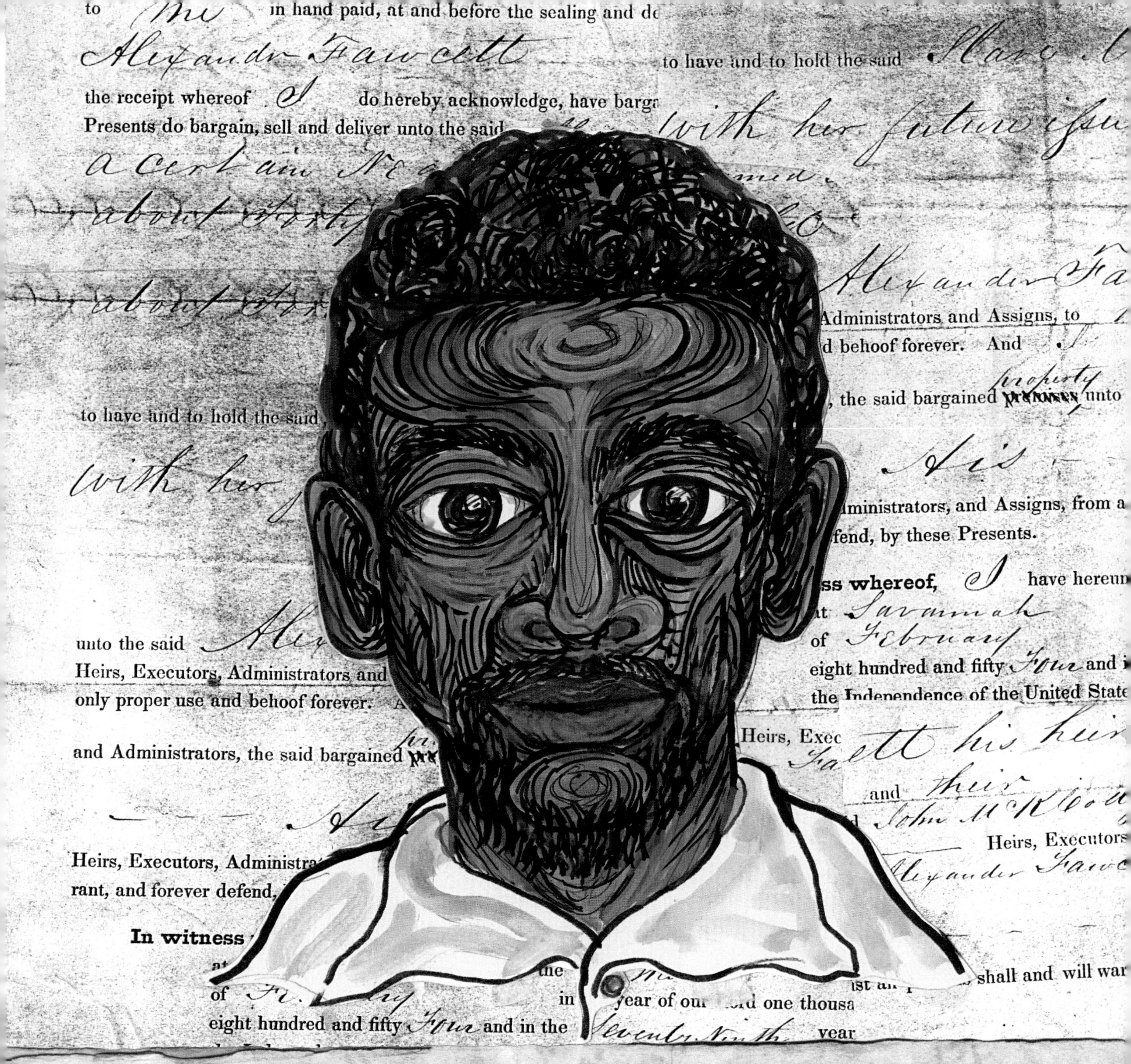

$300 *Stephen, age 32*

Stephen

Mr. Fairchilds apprenticed me
to the carpentry trade.
I work at the Big House
building cabins for the slaves,
sheds for the cattle.

Learning how to work
with measurements and tools
gives me an inner strength.
I seek out the secret life
of each tool.
Building is in my blood.
I feel an independence in building—
a feeling I never got
from picking cotton.

As my skills increased,
the Fairchilds loaned me out
to work on other estates.
The different projects
extend my abilities;
I am able to figure out
complicated building designs,
some that even the foreman cannot.
My skills add to the wealth
of the Fairchildses' estate.

I am permitted
to teach carpentry
to the young slave John.
He helps me in my work
on the estate.
John is like a son
to me and Jane.

I love Jane,
seamstress to the estate.
I built the special
sewing shed for her.
To do our work
we learned words,
names for cloths and woods.
We learned numbers and
measurements.

To teach a slave to read
is a crime.
Secretly, Jane and I
taught each other to read,
helped by my hidden Bible.
Owners of the slaves think
reading would give us
ideas for freedom.
We know that whether we can read
or not,
we all want to be free.

Stephen dreams

I was enslaved
in Central Africa.
In chained coffles
I survived the long walk
to the coast.

My family named me Yerodin,
meaning "Studious."
My father told me
stories of our ancestors—
the stone builders of Zimbabwe.
The University of Timbuktu.
These stories inspired me.

My owners see me
as their property,
following their orders,
doing their bidding.
But through my carpentry
I feel the accomplishment
and pride
of a free man.

I would choose
to design and build
homes for people
in all climates
throughout the world.
And for Jane.

Jane and I
love each other.
We dream
of a proper marriage
in a free land.
Our children then
would not be owned by others,
slaves for life.
They would be *our* children,
free for life.

$300 *Jane, age 28*

Jane

I'm seamstress to Mrs. Fairchilds.
Noted
for my skills with cloth,
I design and sew
all of Mrs. Fairchilds's dresses,
tailor shirts and trousers
for Mr. Fairchilds as well.

I enjoy matching colored cloths,
creating unusual patterns.
This has brought many compliments
to the wearer.
Some deep remembrance
of woven African cloths
lives on in me.

There were so many requests for my
sewing
from Mrs. Fairchilds's friends,
Mr. Fairchilds had Stephen
build a separate shed
as my workplace.

I love Stephen.
He is carpenter to the estate.
He stands tall,
walks like a free man.

Slaves whisper stories they've heard
of runaways,
those who made it.
Heartbreaking stories
of those caught,
returned to slavery,
brutally punished.

Stephen and I have talked
of running away,
getting past patterrollers
and their bloodhounds.
At Fairchildses' grand parties,
after the guests' slave helpers
are no longer needed,
they gather in our cabins,
whispering stories
of slave resistance and runaways.
We sing our slave songs loud
to cover our talk.

One day Stephen and I
will live together.
Free!

Jane dreams

Growing up
in my West African village,
I was precious
to my parents.
They named me Serwaa,
meaning "Jewel."

I was apprenticed as a child
to my family's textile industry.
I worked beside my parents.
My eyes danced
to the making of cloths.
I thought the
spinning, weaving,
the dyeing of fabrics
was a miracle of threads,
threads becoming cloths,
cloths becoming clothes to wear.

One day slave raiders
attacked our village.
My parents were killed
fighting to protect me.
I was captured,
enslaved in America.
I stood naked,
sold on the auction block.

At the estate,
weaving became my salvation.
Working with cloths
became the song
of my hands.

I have grown in artistry
through the clothes I create.
The praise I receive,
I offer as a tribute
to my ancestors.

Stephen and I
treat the young slave John
as our son.
We never lose hope
that we will one day
live free.
I weave these thoughts
into dreamcloths
of Freedom.

$100 *John, age 16*

John

When I was eight years old
I was given as a birthday gift
to Mrs. Fairchilds.

I was born on her brother's plantation
in South Carolina.
He owned more than a hundred slaves—
children born became
the owner's property.
I never knew my mother and father.
We children worked in the fields
like grown-ups.

At the Fairchildses' estate
I tended the cattle.
I carried messages
to the Fairchildses' friends.
I was given a pass
to show the patterrollers.
No Negro could walk out
of the estate without a pass.
He would be brutally beaten.

I'm treated as a son
by seamstress Jane
and carpenter Stephen.
Stephen teaches me
how to work with tools.
I help him with
estate building projects.
I want to be like Stephen—
proud, caring, and intelligent.

Secretly, Stephen and Jane
are teaching me to read and write.
They say, "We'll be free one day!
And you will teach others."
My thoughts of escaping
to freedom
grow stronger every day.

Oh Freedom, Oh Freedom,
Oh Freedom over me!

John dreams

I've learned about Africa
from the slaves
with whom I live.
I've known hardship,
seen cruel treatment,
but I've heard slaves
tell stories of Africa's rich cultures.
Stories of Dahomey,
metal and clay sculptures,
tribal ceremonial masks,
and carvings.

These stories
and the African songs
the elders on the estate
taught us
awakened the artist in me.

Stephen and Jane
saw me drawing with sticks
in the clay earth.
They gave me used papers.
I drew everything—
people, animals, plants.

I hide my art
from my owners.
But I show my work
to the other slaves.
They praise my drawings.
They call me Osere,
a Yoruba name for "Artist."
They say, "We're proud of you!"
That makes me feel good.

I wonder how art
came to me, a slave.
Was it from pictures hung
in the Big House?
Was it from art I saw
in homes I entered
carrying messages?

No matter what work I do
on the estate—
even learning carpentry
from Stephen—
I think of drawing.

I plan one day
to draw freely
from free Negro people.
I will create
loving portraits
of their strength
and beauty.

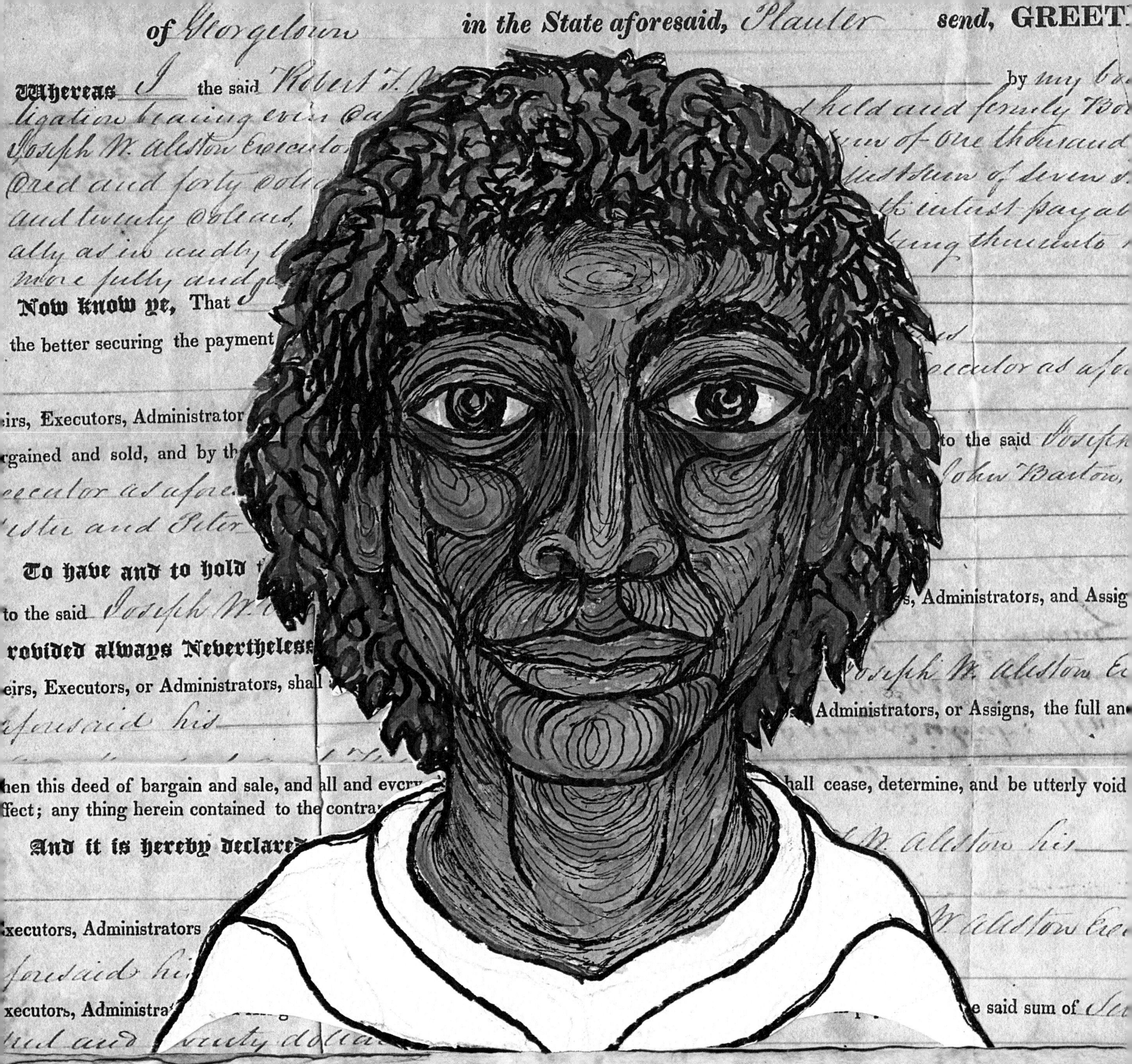

$175 *Athelia, age 42*

Athelia

All we've known as slaves
is work. Work, from dawn to dusk,
in rain, cold, stifling heat.

I'm laundress
for the Fairchilds estate.
I do the cloths,
bed linens, draperies.
I work with seamstress Jane,
washing the clothes she designs.
I'm also a first-rate ironer,
never scorching the cloth,
smoothing pleats and ruffles
in Mrs. Fairchilds's special dresses.

I dress in a plain coarse smock.
At harvest, I work with the men in
the fields.
I drive the cattle to pasture,
milk the Holstein cows,
feed the hogs, clean the sty.

In season,
little Dora and I
gather fruits and berries
for Peggy, the cook.

Little Dora has grown up with me.
She always wants to help.
She is my escape
from drudgery.
We enjoy nibbling the berries,
tasting the fruit.
She calls me by my African name:
Adero, "Life Giver."

As slaves,
we do what our owners
expect and demand of us.
As human beings,
our real lives
are our precious secret.

Athelia dreams

I've never forgotten
how the teaching and learning
in my African village
was by example and voice.

We listened
to the village griot
chanting the history
of our tribe;
we learned stories and songs
that lived on in us.

Peggy and I teach little Dora,
keeping alive
the oral tradition.
When I teach little Dora,
I feel I live up to my name.
Our stories and songs
strengthen our lives.

That's why the elders,
Qush and Mulvina,
lift our spirits
with songs they create.
Songs to the Biblical
stories we've heard.
Songs of our longings
and feelings.

Through all my years
enslaved,
I've listened to
ancestral voices
echoing through
my weariness,
giving me strength
to withstand injustice,
to believe in myself
and survive.

May our songs and stories
keep alive in us
the will to grow in learning.
The longing to be free!

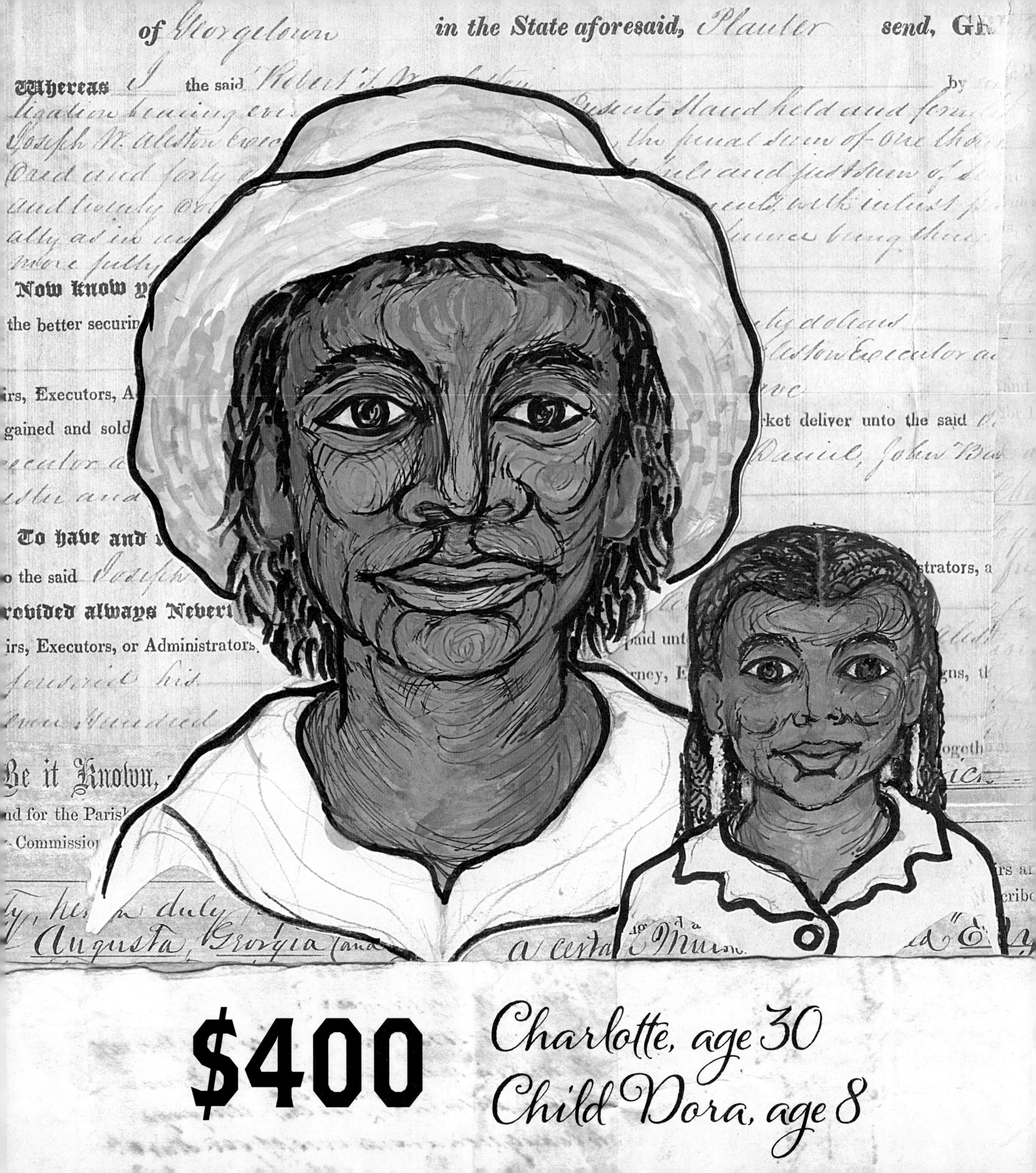
$400
Charlotte, age 30
Child Dora, age 8

Charlotte

As a child in Africa,
I shaped things from river clay—
cups, bowls, animals.
The village potter taught me.
She fired my pieces
in her kiln.

My fingers were never still.
I cut reeds and grasses,
wove them into mats and baskets.

This became my work.
In the Big House shed
I make baskets
shaped for all purposes.
I work hard
to fill the estate's needs
and outside orders
that profit the estate's income
and reputation.

Years ago blacksmith Bacus and I
"jumped the broom"—
the slave custom for marriage.
No legal form for slaves.
No family relation recognized
at a slave auction.

Then, eight years ago,
our daughter was born.
The Fairchilds called her Dora.
Among ourselves we call her Akua.
Akua, "Sweet Messenger."
To Bacus, I am Bisa,
"Greatly Loved."
To us, Bacus is Abena,
"Manly in Bearing."

When I had many basket orders to fill,
the elder slave Athelia
often cared for little Dora.
Our slave family
comes together;
we do all we can
to help each other.

I have taught Dora basket making.
Now,
her baskets sell with mine.

Bacus and I whisper escape plans.
We know the earnings from our work
would support us
in a free land.

Charlotte dreams

The baskets I create
remind me of my family,
my life in Africa.

The owners do not know
that I use my craft
as my way of learning
more about myself.
I am inspired
by the art of my husband, Bacus;
the way he interlaces
strands of metal
for a fence or railing.
This led me to combine
colored rushes
into African patterns.
Accenting the shapes,
bringing distinction
to my baskets.

I am surrounded by
rushes, grasses, straws.
I lose myself
in the endless designs
possible in basketry.

When Bacus and Dora
visit me in the shed,
this confined space,
this close world
returns me
to the open world.
To my village in Africa.

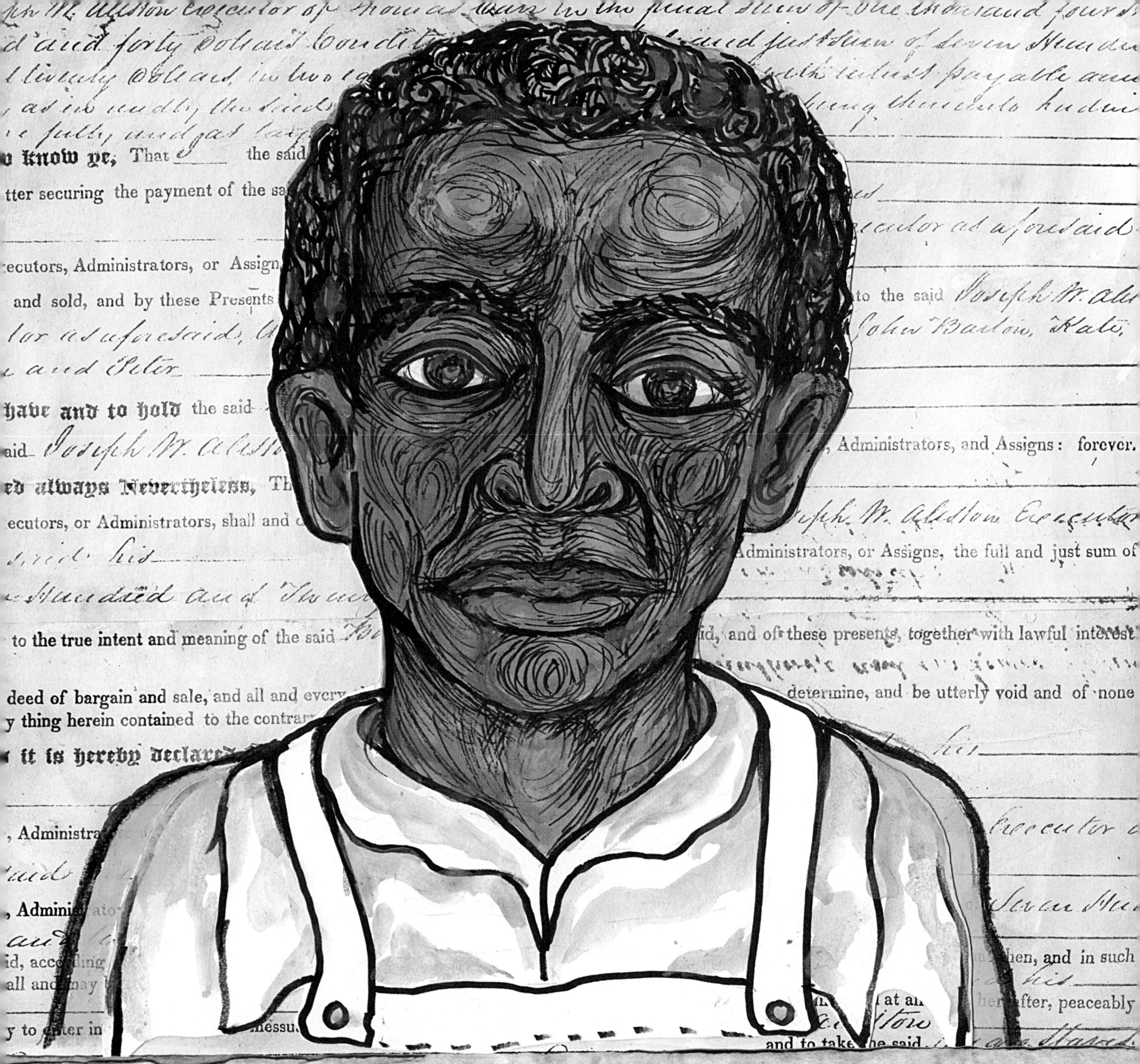

$250 *Bacus, age 34*

Bacus

My wife, Charlotte,
and our daughter, Dora,
keep my hope alive that one day
we will be free.

I was apprenticed to a blacksmith.
I learned to work with metals.
I make the estate's railings and fences.
I make metal parts and objects
for the Big House.
My curved metal patterns
impressed the Fairchildses' guests;
they said my work was as grand
as metal balconies they saw
in New Orleans.

Slaves working at the foundry
during breaks
told tales of runaways.
Knew of slave insurrections
and slave independence in Haiti.

At night I study the stars—
the North Star, the Drinking Gourd.
What chance would I have
with wife and child
of avoiding patterrollers and bloodhounds,
to connect with help
from other slaves and good people
on the road to freedom?
So much planning.
So much wishing.

Now we are up for sale.
I hardly sleep nights.
I have terrible thoughts of separation.
Powerless to keep my family together.
At night I hold Charlotte close.
Dora sleeps quietly
on her straw mat.
Tears of love and hope
fill my eyes.

Bacus dreams

Our owners see us as laborers.
They boast of our skills,
hire us out.
Everything we do
profits their estate.

They do not know that
no matter what the tasks,
our lives are within.
As I work
I think of my wife, Charlotte,
of our daughter, Dora.
Fragile lives!

I work with metals,
from steel to brass.
I master the art
of forging with fire.

With tongs holding hot metal
taken from a glowing furnace,
I pound with a heavy hammer,
an outlet for anger, for rage.
WHAM! WHAM!

Every stroke striking the note:
WHAM! WHAM!
A blow for JUSTICE:
BAM! BAM!
A cry for RESPECT:
BLAM! BLAM!

The beat on the anvil,
a plea for FREEDOM,
calling, calling:
FREEDOM, FREEDOM
OH! OH! FREEDOM!

$100 *Qush, age 60*

Qush

Many years ago
Mulvina and I worked together
on a Louisiana plantation.
Our voices could always be heard
singing, singing, singing.
It was our voices
that brought us together.
We sang to strengthen our spirits.
We cared for each other.
Luckily, we were sold together
to the Fairchildses' estate.

We had a way with animals.
We led their cattle
to green pastures
and still waters.
No matter what the work—
herding the cattle,
tending the garden,
picking cotton—
we sang.

The steady gait of the cattle,
their contented, quiet munching
aroused sentiments of song
within us.
We sang low, thoughtful melodies
to Bible stories we heard
standing in the back
of the Big House
for Sunday church services.
We remembered
the stories of suffering and longing,
of Moses, Joshua, David,
of Jesus and Mary.
Stories like our own.

During the heavy laboring
in the cotton fields,
caring for the garden,
planting rows of vegetables
for the estate,
the tiring daily chores,
Mulvina and I sang together quietly:
"Oh, by and by,
by and by,
I'm gonna lay down
this heavy load."

Qush dreams

The labor of the slaves
made this estate prosperous.
After the hard work
of the day,
I wanted to prosper as well.

Hearing the slaves
singing the songs
Mulvina and I created
reminds me
of the rich musical world
so integral and natural
in African daily
and ceremonial life.

There was so little
of goods or time of our own.
My Yoruba name, Kayode,
means "He Brought Joy."
I thought,
How could I breathe
moments of joy
into our driven lives?

I began making
simple instruments,
flutes of varied tones
from hollow reeds,
seeds in gourds
for rattles.

Drums were forbidden.
Owners feared that messages
could be carried by drum.
We used our bodies
to beat out rhythms.
Clapping hands, slapping sides,
stamping feet.

We made music!
When we stole time
we laughed, we danced.
Moments of joy.
An outlet we seized for survival.
Something of our own.

$100 *Mulvina, age 60*

Mulvina

I'm not as strong
as I once was,
but my singing voice
is as strong as ever.
Still, I work in the fields
picking cotton, planting vegetables.
On my own, I take special care
of Peggy's roots and herbs garden.

Singing gives me strength
for the daily work.
My voice
accompanies me always.

When I am digging
in the garden
I sing, I sing.
Bending over,
seeding the furrows,
weeding the plants,
I sing, I sing.

When Qush and I are together,
we create songs that others love.
We start the song.
Others chant in chorus.
The African song patterns live in us.
We sing out, "This little light of mine,
I'm gonna let it shine."
We can't hold back
the joy of these words.
We sing them over and over
till everyone in the fields
is singing with us,
having made these words
their own.

When Qush and I hear the others
singing our songs,
we feel we've helped them
endure the burden of slavery.
Songs make us never lose hope
we'll be free one day.
Free!

Mulvina dreams

In my African village
I heard the chant of
my African name,
"Niami! Niami!"
It sounded like
the melody that it means.

I've walked a long trail,
a long trail of years
flushed with tears.
Tears of remembrance.

Years of driven labor
have not driven
the ancestral thoughts
out of me.
My memory of teaching—
surrounded by children,
singing songs of our people,
the stories of our history—
lives always with me.

With Dora and John,
I create stories and songs
out of African memories
and longings.
Song shields our hearts from abuse,
draws us together,
strengthens our lives.

I teach them to sing
my song of joy and comfort:
"He's got the whole world
in his hands."
In his hands.

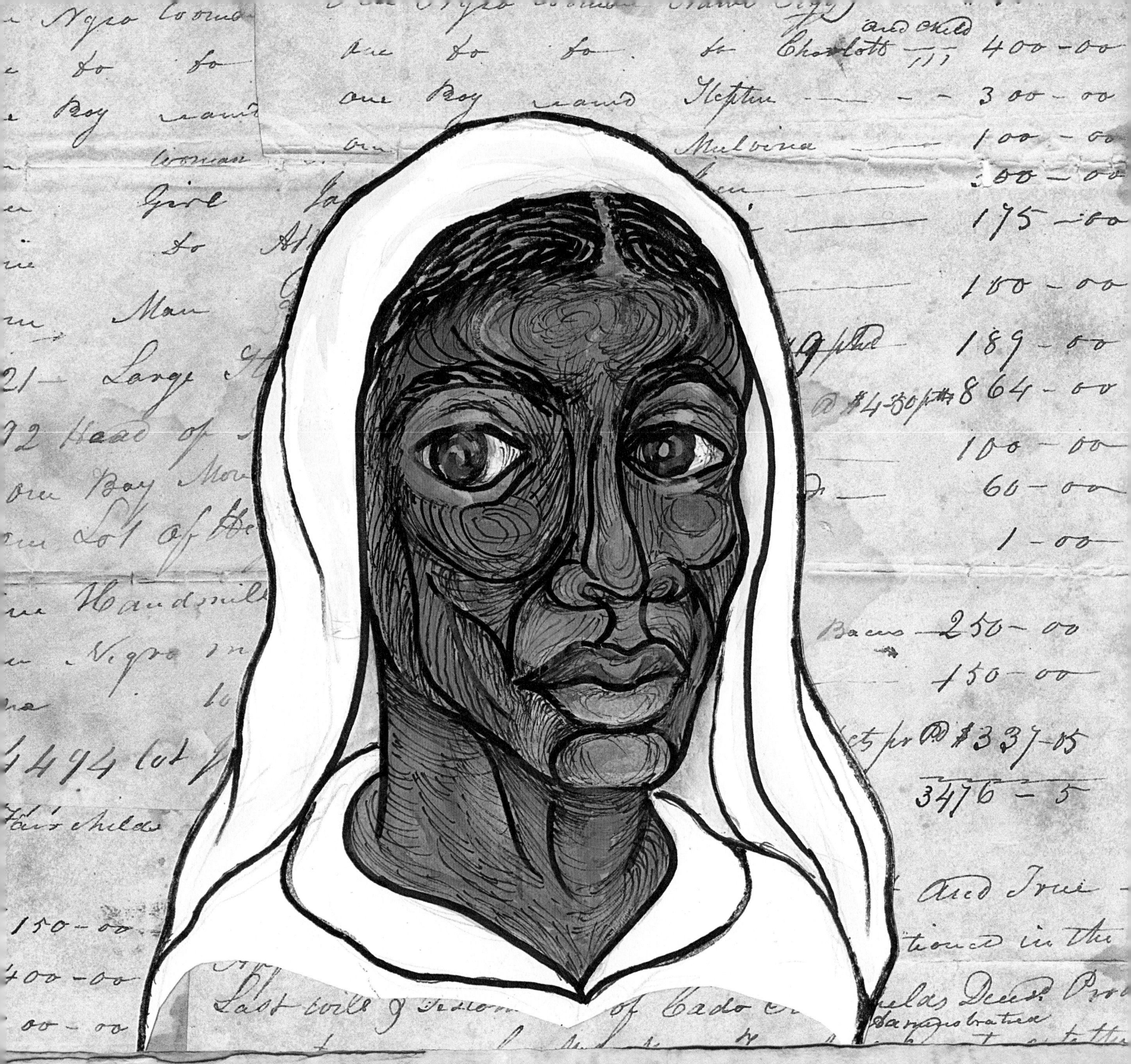

$150 *Betty, age 36*

Betty

I am special flower gardener
to the Fairchildses' estate.
I do the regular cleaning
in the Big House.
Under Mrs. Fairchilds's direction
I set the flower arrangements,
help with all interior décor.
My work has made this house
a model of beauty and comfort.
I'm loaned to other estates
to design their gardens
and bring style to their parlors.

This makes me feel strong within,
to know I have the talent
to decorate a home.
To know my love of nature
reveals to me
inviting garden paths.

Whenever our duties allow,
we gather together
in carefully guarded,
closed quarters.
I choose these times
to speak out.
I tell my brothers and sisters
that it is *our* special talents,
often on loan to others,
that has brought renown
to the Fairchildses' estate.
Our.

My encouraging words
warm every heart.
We embrace one another
in hope and love,
singing softly
the comforting words:
Freedom! Oh, Freedom!

Betty dreams

My Yoruba name,
Temitope, means
"Thanks to God."

As I work
gardening for owners,
I am thinking
if I were free,
I would acquire my own
acres of land.

I would hire
men and women
from cities and farms
to work and study the land
with me.
Earnings from our labor
would benefit all of us,
the workers.

In recognizing our skills and labor,
how can owners say
we are property,
priced and valued like
cotton, cattle, hogs?

The owners say
we have no history.

But we are a people,
though enslaved.
We remember our African cultures,
our traditions, our craftsmanship.
Within us lives this knowledge,
this undefeated pride.

We know we are not slaves.
We are of the human family.
We respect life on earth.
We would share with all
the fruits of our labor.
Our cultivation of the land
is our gift of thanks,
our praise song to Mother Earth.

At An Appraisement Held at the House of
Mrs Fairchilds on the 5th July 1828 to appraise
the Property of the Estate of Cado Fairchild
Dec'd Disposed of his will —

3	2-50	
1	50	
1		
3	00	
11		

One Negro Woman Nam'd Peggy and child — $150-00
to Charlott 400-00
one do do 300-00
one Boy nam'd Neptin 100-00
woman Melvina 300-00
one Girl Jane 175-00
one do Amelia 150-00
one Man Dash 189-00
21 — Large Items @ $9 pha ......
192 Head of Stock Cattle @ $4-50 pha $864-00
one Boy Mou 100-0
one Lot of Hogs 40 H.D Do — 60-0
.... 1-0
One Handmill 250-
one Negro man Named Bacus 150-
one woman Betty
4494 lot Jim Cotton @ 7cts pr @ $33
3476

At An Appraisement Held at the House of Mrs. Fairchilds on the 5th July 1828 to appraise the Property of the Estate of Cado Fairchilds Dec'd, Disposed of his Will—

One Negro Woman named Peggy			$150.00
One	Woman	Charlotte and child	$400.00
One	Boy	named Stephen	$300.00
One	Woman	Mulvina	$100.00
One	Girl	Jane	$300.00
One	Girl	Athelia	$175.00
One	Man	Qush	$100.00
21—Large Steers @ $9 a head			$189.00
192 Head of Stock Cattle at $4.50 per head			$864.00
One Bay Mare			$100.00
One lot of Hogs 40 head @			$60.00
One Handmill			$1.00
One Negro Man named Bacus			$250.00
One	Woman	Betty	$150.00
4494 lot Jin Cotton @ 7 1/2 Cents per pound			$337.05

$3476—

We certify the above to be A Just and True Appraisement of all the Property Mentioned in the Last will & Testament of Cado Fairchilds Deed produced to us by Mrs. Mary Fairchilds.

Administrated to the best of our Judgment—

Wm (William) Avery ⎤
Mr. H. Owens ⎥ Aps.
Lymon Sheppord ⎦

Carl thought about the stars
hanging down like lightbulbs
on long black wires.

In the morning, he set out to discover the answer.

It was the wrong book.

When she came back with the right book,

Carl's heart beat faster with every page he turned.

Each star is a sun. If you traveled into space for many years and then looked back at our sun, it would look dim like a star.
Wowie!

Carl was curious.

He imagined what
would find if he co
travel to the stars.

14

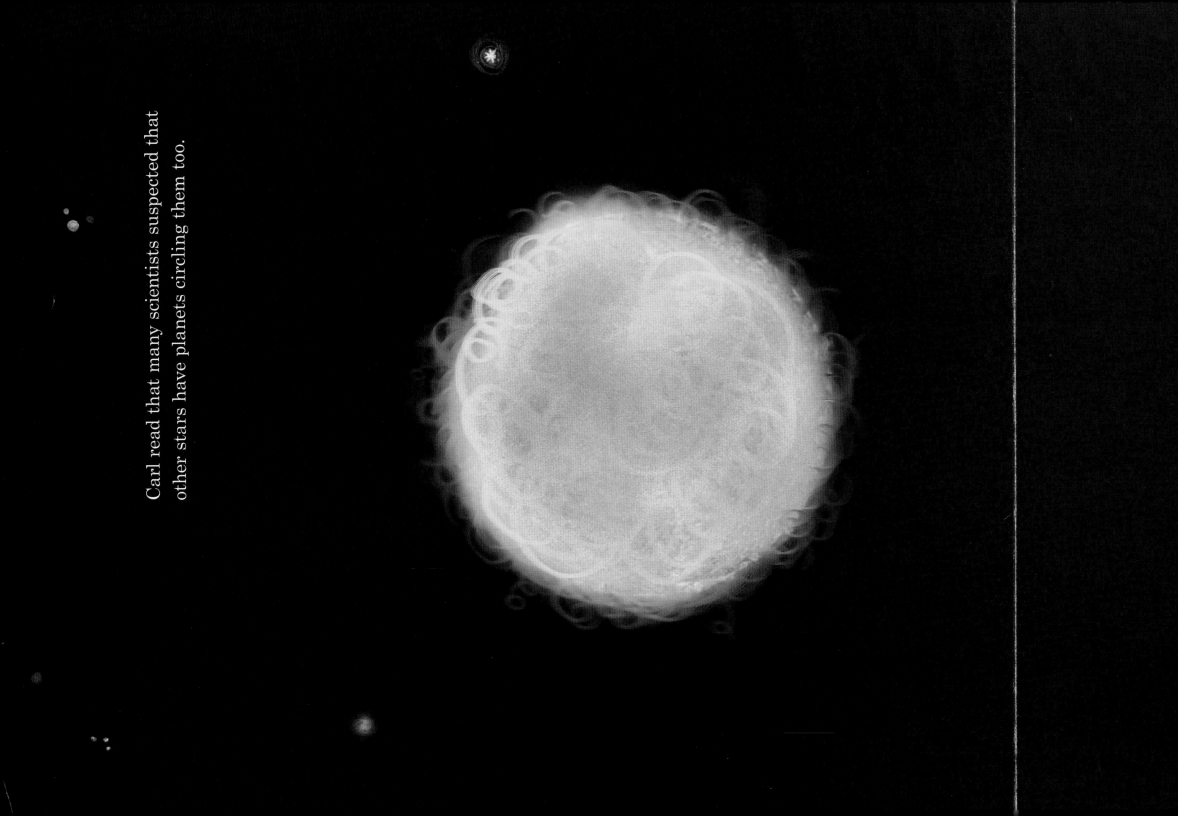

Carl read that many scientists suspected that other stars have planets circling them too.

Our sun is a big ball of fiery gas held together by gravity. Nine planets, including Earth, orbit around it in our solar system.

He read stories written by people who imagined what life might be like on other planets. His favorite character, John Carter, could stand with his arms outstretched and wish himself to Mars . . .

But nothing happened.

Carl set out to learn more. He studied life and space and became . . .

. . . Dr. Carl Sagan.

Carl longed to know what other planets were really like. He worked with other scientists to send mechanical explorers to investigate the planets close to us.

Jupiter

Mariner 9

Venus

Mars

Mariner 2

Pioneer 10

Earth

Viking 1

Mars

They took pictures and gathered data
and sent them back to Earth.

It gave Carl goose bumps to think about what he had
learned about the stars, planets, and the beginnings
of life. He wanted everyone to understand so that they
could feel like a part of the stars as he did.

So he went on television.

The Earth and every living thing are made of star stuff.

The stars made the ingredients of life. Could those ingredients have resulted in life elsewhere too?

Carl and his fellow scientists got ready to launch the *Voyager 1* and *Voyager 2* spacecraft on a grand tour of the outer solar system to gather more pictures and data. After that, they would be bound for the stars.

A marvelous idea gripped Carl.

Voyager 1

Earth

Voyager 2

A message from our world could be attached to each spaceship, like a time capsule, and taken beyond our star.

Music

Heartbeat

Pictures

The twin *Voyagers* rocketed to space carrying their friendly greeting.

They traveled through
our solar system

and continued farther than any other
spaceships have gone before.

A curious man made of star stuff launched a spacecraft on an adventure to explore beyond our neighborhood of planets. As the *Voyagers* continue their journey into interstellar space, they are carried by the imagination of a boy named Carl.

Wowie!

Author's Note

When I was a kid, science was a dull subject to me. It seemed distant and unrelatable. Then, in 1980, something happened that changed how I thought about science: Carl Sagan's *Cosmos: A Personal Voyage* aired on TV. In just thirteen episodes, Dr. Sagan took his audience from the beginning of the universe to the present moment. He explained what scientists understood and suggested what we might understand someday. After I watched it, I began to see the world in a different way. Dr. Sagan's love of his subject was contagious, and the fact that we are made of star stuff gave me a feeling of great joy. Like him, I found myself filled with excitement about what we will discover next!

The most difficult thing about writing a biography of Carl Sagan is that he was so many things: father, explorer, activist, educator, astrophysicist, philosopher, optimist and skeptic, poet and science fiction author. He was at the cutting edge of modern space exploration for over forty-five years: he briefed the Apollo astronauts before their trip to the moon, he speculated about life on other planets, and he helped send unmanned space probes to investigate space. The Voyager mission was the grandest of these projects and embodies both his dedication to scientific discovery and, through the inclusion of the Golden Record, his attitude of goodwill.

Carl Sagan's love of science fiction and his active imagination combined with his knowledge as a scientist gave him a unique voice. He wrote books, papers, and articles, and went on television to explain the great discoveries of science to millions of people all over the globe. His poetic manner of writing and speaking inspired generations to look up at the night sky in wonder.

In this biography I wanted to tell the story of how a boy from Bensonhurst, Brooklyn, New York, became one of the world's most beloved and recognized scientists. How did Carl Sagan go from wondering about the stars as a kid to exploring them through his scientific research?

He said of himself:

> *It has been my enormous luck—I was born at the right time—to have had, to some extent, those childhood ambitions satisfied. I've been involved in the exploration of the solar system, in the most amazing parallel to the science fiction of my childhood . . . For me the continuum from childhood wonder and early science fiction to professional reality has been seamless. It's never been, "Oh gee, this is nothing like what I had imagined." Just the opposite: It's exactly like what I imagined. And I feel so enormously fortunate.*

Through wonder, imagination, and his love for science, Carl knew that he was part of a very big place. He was truly at home in the universe.

Special Thanks

Thank you to my parents, Brian and Marlies Roth, who gave me my first Carl Sagan book when I was a kid, and my critique group, who endured the first dozen drafts of this book—especially Sharon Lovejoy. And thank you to Abigail Samoun and Katherine Jacobs, who saw the potential in this story and who patiently nursed it along. And a big thank you to my husband, Fred, who encouraged me to embark on this story and kept me going.

Notes

Title page There are over fifty galaxies in our local galactic group, and more are being discovered every year.

1 Our Milky Way galaxy is comprised hundreds of billions of stars of which our sun is just one.

2 Our interstellar neighborhood is located in the Orion Arm of the Milky Way galaxy. The planets here are not drawn to scale.

4–5 Carl lived in the Bensonhurst neighborhood of Brooklyn, New York, populated mostly by immigrants. Carl's father worked in a garment factory and Carl's mother stayed home with him and his little sister. Carl was adored by his parents who encouraged his curiosity.

6–7 Carl said, "I remember the end of a long ago perfect day in 1939—a day that powerfully influenced my thinking, a day when my parents introduced me to the wonders of the New York World's Fair."

12–13 Carl said of reading his first book about stars, "the scale of the universe opened up to me . . . There was a magnificence and grandeur, a scale which has never left me." At the time, there were considered to be nine planets in our solar system.

14 By the time Carl was eight, he believed that there must be life in other parts of the universe.

15 This drawing is inspired by an actual childhood drawing that Carl made of his vision of the future when he was eleven years old. His drawing is a part of the Seth MacFarlane Collection of Carl Sagan and Ann Druyan Archive at the Library of Congress.

16–17 Science fiction fueled Carl's curiosity. When he was ten, he loved the Edgar Rice Burroughs series about Mars. As an adult, Carl wrote a science fiction novel called *Contact* that was made into a movie.

19 Carl went to the University of Chicago and the University of California, Berkeley, and graduated with a Ph.D at the age of twenty-six.

20–21 Carl played a part in almost every NASA space exploration mission and loved the surprise of new discoveries. He said, "To see the first close up images of a world never before known this moment is one of the greatest joys in the life of an interplanetary scientist." Pictured here are *Mariner 2*, which was the first space probe to make a planetary encounter with Venus, *Mariner 9*, which was the first to orbit Mars, and *Pioneer 10*, which made the first mission to Jupiter. Note that Carl's computer screen would have been in black and white. I colored it to make a visual connection between the screen and the *Viking 1* landing.

22–23 Carl felt strongly that people should be scientifically literate. He appeared on the popular *Johnny Carson Show* twenty-six times; his television series *Cosmos* was watched by at least 500 million people around the globe and won the Peabody Medal.

24 Carl wanted people to understand that we are not only part of this world and in this cosmos, but we and our world are actually made of the same organic matter as stars. The stars you see up in the sky are not just twinkling lights—we are related to them.

25 The *Voyagers* used a method of slingshotting themselves through space called gravity assist. Their paths in the illustration have been simplified.

26–27 Carl headed a team of people to create a message from Earth that would be included on *Voyager 1* and *2*. They tried to get a wide representation of the people and life on Earth. Carl included music that conveyed loneliness and a longing to connect. The golden disks also had a recording made by Carl's six-year-old son, Nick, who said, "Greetings from the children of planet Earth." The heartbeat of Carl's future wife, Ann Druyan, was also recorded as she fell in love—with Carl. Ann has said that the records were a message to other possible beings. "We want to be citizens of the cosmos. We want you to know about us."

28–29 In 1990, Carl requested for *Voyager 1*'s cameras to take one final picture before they were turned off forever—this one of Earth. This picture is called the Pale Blue Dot and Carl wrote a famous essay with the same title. The *Voyager* space probes are now the farthest man-made objects from Earth. On September 12, 2013, NASA confirmed that *Voyager 1* became the first man-made object to leave our solar system and enter interstellar space. They will likely continue to travel for billions of years.

Bibliography and Sources

The Carl Sagan Portal: carlsagan.com.

The Cosmos: A Personal Voyage. Directed by Adrian Malone. PBS, 1980.

Davidson, Keay. *Carl Sagan: A Life*. New York: John Wiley & Sons, 1999.

Head, Tom, ed. *Conversations with Carl Sagan*. Jackson, Mississippi: University Press of Mississippi, 2006.

NASA's Carl Sagan page: solarsystem.nasa.gov/people/profile. cfm?Code=SaganC.

Poundstone, William. *Carl Sagan: A Life in the Cosmos*. New York: Henry Holt & Company, 1999.

Radiolab, "Carl Sagan and Ann Druyan's Ultimate Mix Tape": npr.org/2010/02/12/123534818/carl-sagan-and-ann-druyans-ultimate-mix-tape.

Sagan, Carl, et al. *Murmurs of Earth: The Voyager Interstellar Record*. New York: Random House, 1978.

Sagan, Carl. *Cosmos*. New York: Random House, 1980.

Sagan, Carl. *Pale Blue Dot: A Vision of the Human Future in Space*. New York: Random House, 1994.

Sagan, Carl. "Wonder and Skepticism," keynote address at the CSICOP Conference, Seattle, WA, June 23–26. *Skeptical Inquirer* 19, no. 1, January/February 1995.

Sagan, Carl. *The Demon-Haunted World: Science as a Candle in the Dark*. New York: Ballantine Books, 1996.

Sagan, Carl: *Billions and Billions: Thoughts on Life and Death at the Brink of the Millenium*. New York: Ballentine Books, 1997.

Spangenburg, Ray and Kit Moser. *Carl Sagan: A Biography*. New York: Prometheus Books, 2009.

Voyager Golden Record: goldenrecord.org.

Source Notes

Endpapers "Imagination will often carry us to worlds that never were, but without it we go nowhere." Sagan, *Cosmos*.

23 "The very matter that makes us up was generated long ago and far away in red giant stars." *The Cosmos: A Personal Voyage*, "Travels in Space and Time."

24 "The earth and every living thing are made of star stuff." *The Cosmos: A Personal Voyage*. "Travels in Space and Time."

30 "It has been my enormous luck . . ." Sagan, "Wonder and Skepticism."

31 "I remember the end of a long ago perfect day . . ." Sagan, *Billions and Billions*.

31 "the scale of the universe opened up to me . . ." Davidson, *Carl Sagan: A Life*.

31 "To see the first close up images of a world never before known . . ." *The Cosmos: A Personal Voyage*, "Time Traveler's Tales."

31 "We want to be citizens of the cosmos . . ." Radiolab.